T0197504

By Cora Elizabeth Deitz

Charlie
Finds a way

Illustrated by Mariam Muhammad

Archway Publishing books may be ordered through booksellers or by contacting:

Archway Publishing
1663 Liberty Drive
Bloomington, IN 47403
www.archwaypublishing.com
844-669-3957

Because of the dynamic nature of the Internet, any web addresses or links contained in this book may have changed since publication and may no longer be valid. The views expressed in this work are solely those of the author and do not necessarily reflect the views of the publisher, and the publisher hereby disclaims any responsibility for them.

ISBN: 978-1-6657-4323-5 (sc)
ISBN: 978-1-6657-4325-9 (hc)
ISBN: 978-1-6657-4324-2 (e)

Library of Congress Control Number: 2023908104

Print information available on the last page.

Archway Publishing rev. date: 05/15/2023

Charlie was a small bear,
Or so he thought.
So small he had a talent
For things like getting lost

In airports, hotels,
On beaches and whatnot.

2

You see, Charlie's not your average

Little, cuddly teddy bear,
At least, according to his friend, Lilly,
Who said he was "quite rare".

Of course, traveling could sometimes
Make a bear's life harder.

But Charlie found out he loved
Being the bear of a pilot's daughter.

4

He was h^ap^py to have a friend like Lilly
Who taught him new experiences
Weren't scary, not really!

He'd seen Paris in France,
And the Great Wall of China,
He'd been from Los Angeles, California
To North AND South Carolina!

Barcelona in Spain

And Milan in Italy!

Next Tokyo in Japan

Then big, bright
New York City!

He saw a pyramid in Egypt,

And a volcano in Greece!

A cathedral in Moscow,

The adventures never ceased

Africa, Australia,
and India too.

Cities like Rome
and Timbuktu!

ROME

AUSTRALIA

Every place Charlie went
Held something new.

Sure, even Lilly
(The bravest girl he knew)
sometimes got scared,
Just like me and you.

But home is where the heart is
And from Paris to Rome
No matter how far
This little bear roamed

He knew that deep down,
Where Lilly was, was his home.

16

And Lilly got a bit older,
As they traveled the world
Just a brave little bear
And an adventurous little girl.

There was one fateful day
In an airport cafe
When Lilly and our Charlie Bear
Met a boy who seemed afraid.

His family was moving to America,
And that made him feel scared.

That's when Lilly looked
At our brave little bear
And remembered what it was like
When she, too, had felt scared.

She thought to herself,
"I was once afraid too,

But now I love traveling!
I know just what to do."

She gave Charlie a hug and a kiss.
He was the best teddy bear,
Who, of course, she would miss.

But she looked at the boy and said
"You should have this."

So that is how Charlie
Met young Benjamin,

And knew straight away
They'd be the best of friends,
Traveling from New Zealand
All the way to Switzerland.

Charlie couldn't wait to see the **world**
All over again!

By train, or boat, or bus, or plane,
Charlie and his friends

Always found a way
To overcome their fears
And Remember to...

Be
Brave

SPAIN

FRANCE

AMERICA

ITALY

AFRICA

AFRICA

CHARLIE'S TRAVELS

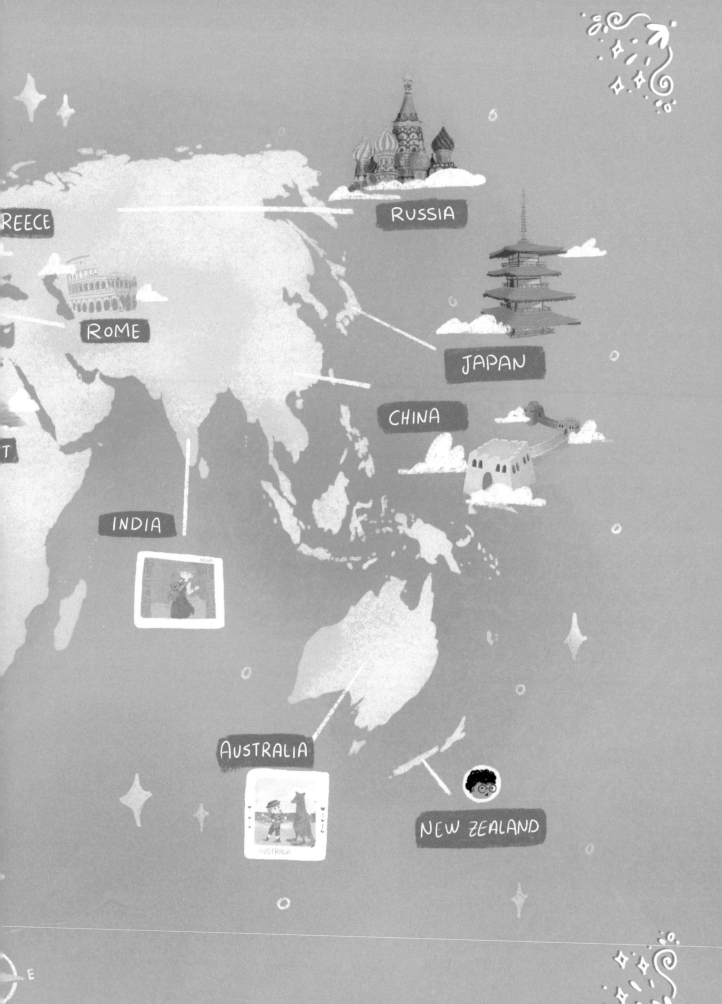

Cora Elizabeth Deitz grew up in the small town of Lenoir, North Carolina. After traveling the world as an English teacher and a yoga instructor, she is dedicating her time to teaching children the lessons she learned on her journeys - Be brave. Be kind. Be YOU.

Printed in the United States
by Baker & Taylor Publisher Services